Little Frog and the
Frog Olympics

by Martin Waddell
Illustrated by Trevor Dunton

2

It was Frog Olympics
Day at the Pond.
Little Frog was
excited.

"I'm going to win a gold medal!"
Little Frog told
his Auntie.

"The other Frogs are all bigger than you, Little Frog," Auntie Frog said.

Splash-splash-splash-splash.
Little Frog finished last.
Big frogs swim faster than
little frogs can.

"I might win the Three-legged Hop,"
Little Frog said to Auntie Frog.
"But I've no one to hop with."

Auntie Frog got Bull Frog to help
Little Frog.

Bull Frog fell over Little Frog's leg, and they lost.

"I could try the Frog Wrestle,"
Little Frog said.

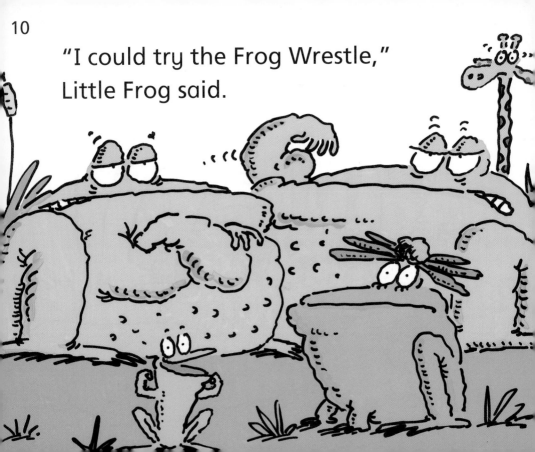

But Little Frog lost to Fat Frog!

"I never win!" Little Frog said,
and he sat down and cried.

"Try the Frog Jump, Little Frog,"
Auntie Frog said.
"Big frogs jump higher than little
frogs can!" Little Frog said.

Little Frog tried.

Oooooch!

Little Frog won!